December 2023

To Joseph + Indora —

Happy Chanukah!

Love Babi + Zaida

The Chanukah Blessing

By Peninnah Schram

Illustrated by Jeffrey Allon

UAHC Press • New York

To my grandson, Ilan Moshe Zafrany
PS

To my father, Michael Allon,
who shared my first Chanukahs with me
JA

Library of Congress Cataloging-in-Publication Data

Schram, Peninnah
Chanukah blessing / Peninnah Schram ; illustrated by Jeffrey Allon.
p. cm.
Summary: A mysterious visitor rewards a poor family for showing
him hospitality on the fifth night of Chanukah.
ISBN 0-8074-0733-X
[1. Hanukah—Fiction.] I. Allon, Jeffrey, ill. II. Title.

PZ7.S3774 Ch 2000
[E]—dc21
00-036426

A stranger came to a small town on the fifth night of Chanukah. It was cold and wintry. The snow had stopped falling. As the stranger walked, his footsteps made a deep impression in the sparkling snow, and the crunching sound broke the quietness all around him.

The stranger walked slowly past many houses, looking careful-ly at each one as he passed. What was he looking for?

"Aha!" he called out softly, and in the coldness of the air his breath formed a puff of white smoke. "Here is the house I'm looking for." And he stopped at a certain cottage.

It was a tiny house compared to the others in the town. There was nothing to make it stand out, except for . . .

The stranger knocked gently at the cottage door. In a moment, the door opened a crack, and behind the door stood a woman.

"What do you wish?" asked the woman.

"I am a stranger here in town. And it is a cold wintry night. The synagogue is dark and cold because everyone has already left to return to their homes to celebrate Chanukah. May I come in to warm myself at your stove?" asked the stranger.

"Oh yes, yes, come in. Sholom aleichem. It would give me great honor to invite you in to join our celebration.

To be alone, even in the synagogue, is not right on this night. Come in quickly, for the cold is bitter and enters quickly too," responded the woman with a wave of her arm, offering her hospitality without hesitation.

In the small room that the stranger entered sat five children, three older and two much younger. They were sitting close to the stove. They were trying to get warm, but there was also a sense of impatience, each one staring at the stove wishing they were able to see inside it through the bricks.

"Mama, who is there?" asked the oldest youngster.

"Mama, Mama, *when* will it be ready?" another child asked.

"When, Mama?" echoed the youngest.

"Right away! Right away!" answered the mama as she welcomed in the stranger, taking his heavy fur-lined black coat and hat. She motioned him to come nearer to the stove and, at the same time, gestured for the children to make room for the guest.

All the children stared at the guest, thinking to themselves: Who is this stranger? Why is he here? Who invited him to share our *latke-kugel* when there's hardly enough for us? Looking at the children's faces, the stranger read their thoughts. But the youngest, little Rivkele, didn't share those thoughts. She was just happy to have more company. She ran over to the guest with open arms, calling out, "Tell me a story!"

"In a short while, my little bird," replied the stranger with a smile. And when he smiled, it seemed as if his long white beard grew twice as wide and formed many shapes.

In the meantime, the mama had opened the oven, and the room was instantly filled with the delicious aroma of a large baked potato latke—a *latke-kugel*—all brown and crisp. The mama took the *latke-kugel* carefully out of the oven with a long wooden-handled paddle and placed it on the table. The children gathered around the table, eyeing their favorite Chanukah food. They reached out with their hands as if to touch the pan—as if to scoop the whole *latke-kugel* into their mouths—the littler ones imitating the bigger ones.

The *latke-kugel* was big enough for three, maybe four people, to eat. But now it would have to be divided into seven portions.

The mama found her place at the table, again remembering to welcome the stranger to the Chanukah meal. First came the blessing, which the children wanted to recite quickly, but the mama said it very slowly, and the children had to slow down. All this time, the stranger watched each one in turn, smiling mysteriously.

Finally, the mama began to cut the *latke-kugel*, dividing most of it equally, except for one piece that was bigger than the rest, and one especially smaller. Each child hoped the biggest piece would "fall" onto his or her plate, but it was the stranger, the guest, who was served first, and with the biggest piece of *latke-kugel*. Now the children hoped that they would not "win" the smallest piece, but mama saved that one for herself. Most of the children ate the *latke-kugel* slowly, wanting to make it last as long as possible, but some ate it quickly, hoping that somehow more would appear. After eating, they sang Chanukah songs while they cleared the table. Then one of the children got the dreidel. The others brought some nuts to the table, and the dreidel game began.

After a while, Rivkele turned her attention again to the guest and asked, "Can you tell me a story now?"

"Gladly," replied the guest. "But first let me tell you why I came to this house. As you see, I am a stranger in this town. And arriving too late to go to *shul*, I went searching for a Jewish home. Well, on Chanukah, I knew I could recognize a Jewish home by the menorah in the window. When I saw your beautiful menorah, I knew this was the house I wanted to visit."

"Beautiful? It's not even a menorah! It's—potatoes! A potato menorah!" cried out the oldest child, not hiding his shame.

"It's all we have," replied the mama. "We cannot afford to buy a real menorah made of metal. Maybe next year . . ." and her voice faded away. The stranger saw a tear fall into her open hand as if she had held it there—open—in midair just to catch the tear.

"But that is *why* I came here to this house," continued the stranger. "This is a menorah as real as any other made of silver or gold. It fulfills the mitzvah of burning oil with a wick to celebrate our *yom tov*—but it is a menorah filled also with love of mitzvah. When you have money, then it's easy to buy a menorah. But you and your mama had to make your menorah. You chose the potatoes with great care. You cut open the potatoes carefully. You counted how many halves you needed for five wicks and a *shammas*. And you put your menorah in the window for the world to see. *Nu?* What can be more beautiful than that?" Then, turning to the youngest children, he said, "So now, little ones, I will tell you a story of wonder and light."

And the stranger sat near the stove with the children and the mama around him and he told the story of the Maccabees and their fight for freedom and how they found and lit the cruse of oil in the restored menorah to rededicate the Temple in Jerusalem.

And they heard how a miracle happened when the little bit of oil, enough for only one night, lasted for eight nights.

When the stranger had finished the story, he added, "And since this is the fifth night of Chanukah, it is a tradition to give Chanukah *gelt.*" To each child he gave shiny coins, each according to his or her age. And to the mama, he gave his blessing.

The next morning, when the family awoke, the stranger was gone. The children counted their Chanukah *gelt* again and again, feeling happier than they had in a long time. The mama went to the flour barrel, thinking how she had only a few cupfuls left for a meager loaf of bread. But when she lifted the cover, to her surprise, she found the barrel full. And mixed in with the flour she also found some gold coins. When the mama went to see how many potatoes she had left for the *latke-kugels* for the next three nights of Chanukah, she discovered overflowing bags full of potatoes.

The mama laughed gently as she said, almost to herself, "Our guest must have been Elijah the Prophet."

All day long the younger children played in the snow, and the older ones went sliding and skating on the frozen river. Unlike other times, the rabbis said not a word to deny the children this pleasure on Chanukah, because, after all, they were busy with other holiday matters. The stranger, who truly was Elijah the Prophet, witnessed all of this. As he walked along the river, Elijah smiled and laughed good-naturedly, his eyes twinkling all the while.

That night, the mama and the children prepared six halves of potatoes and a seventh half for the *shammas*. They scooped out the centers, poured the oil carefully into each hollow, and placed a wick into each. Lighting the *shammas*, they joyfully sang the blessings and lit the six wicks. On this night, and on all the remaining nights of Chanukah, they enjoyed eating their mama's wonderful and more plentiful *latke-kugel* while they watched, with renewed pride, the dancing lights of their precious potato menorah and remembered their Chanukah blessing.

・ AUTHOR'S NOTE ・

Elijah the Prophet

Elijah the Prophet, the master of miracles, is the most popular hero in Jewish folklore. He is called Eliyahu HaNavi in Hebrew. A prophet in Israel during the reigns of Ahab and Ahaziah (ninth century B.C.E.), he is also associated with the coming of the Messiah. However, as a character in folktales, Elijah excels in miracles. Traditionally, he is most closely associated with Passover. However, Elijah appears throughout the year, in folklore, in rituals, at holidays, and at every life-cycle event, protecting and performing miracles to help those in need. Elijah often appears in disguise in order to witness people's actions and words. He then rewards the worthy and brings about justice.

Elijah the Prophet is my favorite folklore character because he was the main character in my earliest remembered story. When I was a young child, I used to ask my father over and over to tell me the story about Elijah who would "whistle" every time he granted a wish or withdrew his magical "gift." That story had a profound influence in shaping my life. I discovered that my love for Elijah stories and the themes most often found in them (especially hospitality) stems from that first remembered story.

The Chanukah Blessing is an original story created by my weaving together scraps of memories, remnants of recalled dialogue, recollections of beloved people, and timeless Elijah folktale motifs—together with my mama's delicious Chanukah latke-kugels.

Mama's Latke-Kugel

4–6 large potatoes
2–3 eggs
¼ cup matzah meal
1 tablespoon wheat germ
1 teaspoon salt (more or less)
1 tablespoon honey
Oil for frying—or a mixture of oil and margarine

Peel and grate the potatoes, and drain the liquid through the sieve into a bowl, but reserve the potato starch at the bottom of the bowl after pouring off the liquid. Then mix the eggs, matzah meal, wheat germ, salt, and honey with the grated potatoes and potato starch. Add more matzah meal if the mixture is too loose.

Heat oil in a large frying pan. When the oil is hot, pour the entire potato mixture into the pan and brown over medium heat. Carefully lift the sides and bottom with a spatula to make sure there is enough oil. Lower the heat, and cover the pan.

After the latke-kugel has a crisp crust and is set and partially cooked, then carefully slide the latke-kugel onto a plate larger than the pan, using a spatula to help detach the crust from the pan. Place another large plate gently over the latke-kugel, and invert them so that the uncooked side of the latke-kugel is now on the bottom of the second plate, with the browned crust on top. Slide the latke-kugel carefully back into the frying pan (add more oil if necessary) and raise the heat. After browning the bottom crust, cover the pan, lower the heat and cook the latke-kugel until it is cooked through thoroughly. Keep checking so that the bottom doesn't burn. About 30-45 minutes.

When cooked, remove the entire latke-kugel onto a large plate and serve by cutting into wedges.

If you prefer baking, pour oil and then the entire potato mixture into a baking pan (round or square or rectangle). Bake in a 350 degree oven for about 1 hour or until there is a crisp crust around the sides and bottom of the latke-kugel.

Enjoy!

Glossary

Chanukah—Hebrew for "dedication." Refers to that time in the year 165 B.C.E. when Judah and his army, called the Maccabees, defeated the army of the tyrant Antiochus IV Epiphanes and recaptured the holy Temple in Jerusalem after three years of fighting. Antiochus's soldiers had defiled the Temple and established a center for the worship of Antiochus himself and other pagan idols. Judah and his brethren purified the Temple and rededicated it to the service of God. The exploits of the Maccabees may be found in a variety of sources, from the apocryphal books of Maccabees 1 and 2, to Philo and the Rabbis of the Talmud. The popular legend of the miraculous cruse of oil is actually attributed to the talmudic Rabbis, who lived centuries after the Maccabees.

dreidel—Spinning top used during Chanukah. It has four sides, each displaying one of the four Hebrew letters *nun, gimmel, hei,* and *shin.* These letters represent the Hebrew phrase *Nes gadol hayah sham,* meaning "A great miracle happened there." The miracle refers to the cruse of oil found by the Maccabees when they won Jerusalem from the hands of Antiochus's armies. Thereupon they entered the holy Temple, which had been defiled by Antiochus's troops. As they went about cleansing the Temple, they discovered a small cruse that seemed to hold just enough oil to burn for one night. Miraculously, however, the oil burned for eight nights. Hence, according to this tradition, we celebrate Chanukah for eight nights because of "the great miracle that happened there."

gelt—Yiddish for "money." It is traditional to give Chanukah gelt as a token gift, especially to children, and to give Chanukah gelt for charity.

kugel—Yiddish for "pudding." It usually refers to a pudding made either with potatoes or with noodles.

latke—Yiddish for "potato pancake," one of the traditional foods prepared by Eastern European Jews for Chanukah. The latke is cooked in oil and so reminds us of the oil found by the Maccabees, which burned miraculously for eight nights.

latke-kugel—A large, thick potato pancake that needs to be cut in squares or wedges.

Maccabees—Name given to the heroes of Chanukah; namely, the sons of Mattathias and their followers. Mattathias had five sons: Judah, Yochanan, Eleazar, Jonathan, and Simon. The term *maccabee* usually is explained in one of two ways. The name represents a transliteration of the Greek word for hammer and describes the manner in which Judah and his troops would launch a lightning strike upon Antiochus's troops, like a hammer. It is also believed to represent the first letters of the Hebrew expression translated as "Who is like you, O Lord, among the mighty?"

Menorah—A special candelabra used specifically for Chanukah. It holds nine candles or wicks in oil: one for each night of Chanukah and one for the *shammas*.

mitzvah—Hebrew for "precept," "commandment," or "religious duty." Sometimes understood as a "good deed."

shammas—The ninth candle used to kindle each of the other Chanukah candles as they are lit on each of the eight nights of Chanukah. No other candle can be used for the purpose of kindling the others. Shammash is the Hebrew pronunciation of shammas.

sholom aleichem—Yiddish for "peace be unto you." A greeting. In Hebrew, "shalom aleichem."

shul—Yiddish for "synagogue."

yom tov—Hebrew for "festival" or "holy day." Used in Yiddish too, but pronounced yontif.

More Elijah Stories

Frankel, Ellen. *The Classic Tales: 4,000 Years of Jewish Lore.* Northvale, NJ: Jason Aronson Inc., 1989.

Goldin, Barbara Diamond. *Journeys with Elijah: Eight Tales of the Prophet.* Paintings by Jerry Pinkney. New York: Gulliver Books/Harcourt Brace & Company, 1999.

Jaffe, Nina. *The Mysterious Visitor: Stories of the Prophet Elijah.* New York: Scholastic Press, 1997

Klapholtz, Yisroel Yaakov. *Stories of Elijah the Prophet.* 4 vols. Vol. 1, Jerusalem: Feldheim. Vols. 2–4, Bnei Brak, Israel: Pe'er Hasefer. 1970–1979.

Sadeh, Pinhas. *Jewish Folktales.* Trans. Hillel Halkin. New York: Doubleday, 1989

Schram, Peninnah. *Jewish Stories One Generation Tells Another.* Northvale, NJ: Jason Aronson Inc., 1987.

Schram, Peninnah. *Tales of Elijah the Prophet.* Northvale, NJ: Jason Aronson Inc., 1991.

Schwartz, Howard. *Elijah's Violin & Other Jewish Fairy Tales.* New York: Oxford University Press, 1994.

Schwartz, Howard. *Miriam's Tambourine: Jewish Folktales from Around the World.* New York: Oxford University Press, 1988.

Weinreich, Beatrice. *Yiddish Folktales.* Trans. Leonard Wolf. New York: Pantheon, 1988.